THE RIVEN TREE

ROBBY KAUTZ

Archway Publishing books may be ordered through booksellers or by contacting:

Archway Publishing
1663 Liberty Drive
Bloomington, IN 47403
www.archwaypublishing.com
1 (888) 242-5904

Because of the dynamic nature of the Internet, any web addresses or links contained in this book may have changed since publication and may no longer be valid. The views expressed in this work are solely those of the author and do not necessarily reflect the views of the publisher, and the publisher hereby disclaims any responsibility for them.

Any people depicted in stock imagery provided by Getty Images are models, and such images are being used for illustrative purposes only.
Certain stock imagery © Getty Images.

ISBN: 978-1-4808-6674-4 (sc)
ISBN: 978-1-4808-6675-1 (hc)
ISBN: 978-1-4808-6673-7 (e)

Print information available on the last page.

Archway Publishing rev. date: 05/15/2019

To my siblings: Steve, Ruti, Paul, Dave and Dan,
and to my husband Steve, and our children, Stephanie and David.

"Come to Me, all who are weary and heavy laden,
and I will give you rest." Matthew 11:28
Jesus of Nazareth

INTRODUCTION:

Trauma is often a forbidden topic. As a result, many trauma victims remain unaware of its effect in their lives, and they come to believe something is wrong with them. Using story and pictures, *The Riven Tree* speaks to the heart simply and gently, providing insight into the effects of trauma. While not specific to any one religion or philosophy, it seeks to answer the question of the heart, "What does God think of me?"

Once upon a warm autumn day, a small brown acorn lay in the shade of a giant oak. Surrounded by her brothers and sisters and listening to the song of the wind, the little acorn was content to nestle in the comfort of her mother's freshly fallen leaves.

Looking up, she knew that as long as she could see her mother's tall trunk and strong branches, all would be well.

Gazing at her mother's leaves dancing in the breeze, Acorn saw a squirrel look down at her. His eyes fixed on her as he jumped from branch to branch, then raced down her mother's trunk.

He scampered over to her and sat on his haunches. Acorn held her breath. She had seen squirrels take some of her brothers and sisters away, but, she knew not where. She wanted to stay right where she was, sheltered in her mother's freshly fallen leaves.

As she lay in squirrel's shade, Acorn shook with fear. The creature's beady eyes darted back and forth. Then he scooped her up, set her firmly between his teeth, and raced away. Acorn bumped up and down as squirrel carried her further and further away from all she loved. She pushed and wriggled, but, she could not break free. With all her strength, she willed herself to return to the safety of her mother, but all in vain.

When squirrel raced into an open meadow, everything in Acorn cried, *"No, no, no!"*

Finally squirrel's footsteps slowed, then stopped. Acorn shivered, *Where has squirrel taken me?*

Squirrel spit her to the ground and pushed her into a small hole. Looking up at the blue cloudless sky, Acorn helplessly watched squirrel swoosh dirt over her. Too soon, the hole was filled, and soil and darkness surrounded her. Then all was silent.

Acorn's thoughts raced. *Where's my mother? Why did squirrel take me from her? What will happen to me now?*

The days shortened and cooled. Pressed on all sides in the hard ground, Acorn missed lying in the comfort of her mother's freshly fallen leaves. Day after day she wondered, *Will I ever be set free?*

Winter settled in and snow covered the ground. In the cold, dark silence, she dreamed of her mother's tall trunk and strong branches, the song of the birds, and the warm sunshine.

When the last bit of snow had melted, and winter-brown grass covered the meadow, Acorn woke. As the days lengthened and warmed, a taproot slowly grew inside her hard brown shell. One spring morning, it became too large, and her shell cracked and split apart. Creeping down through the crack, the taproot sprouted leggy roots that grew in search of water. Earthworms softened the dirt, making it easy for her to grow. Acorn's heart filled with anticipation. It was time to leave her cramped, dark hole. But how? And where?

A busy earthworm tunneling a path tickled her roots. Maybe he knew his way around.

"Excuse me sir, my roots are spreading and I need to grow. Which way should I go?"

"Up, go up!" Earthworm said with authority as he squirmed past.

Trusting Earthworm's advice, up and up Acorn pushed. Finally, one morning she gave a last heroic push, and her tiny stem peeped out of the ground.

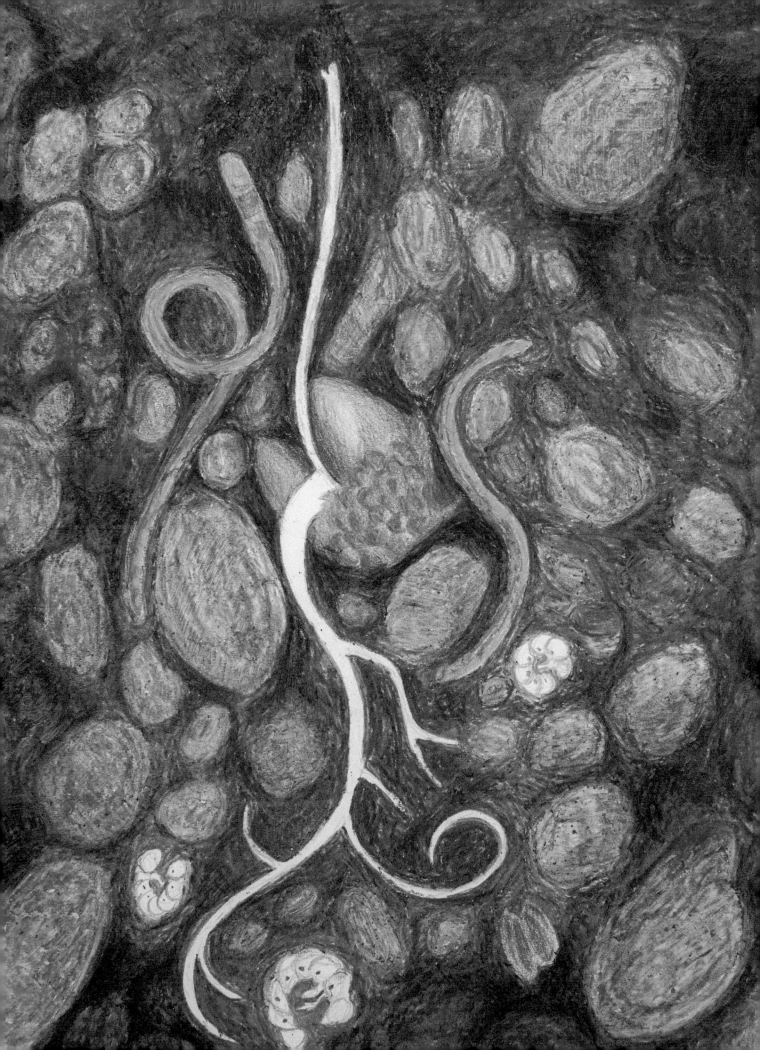

Eagerly breathing in the fresh spring air, Acorn felt reborn. She wanted this moment to last forever. The sun in the clear blue sky warmed her. Looking around, she saw that her new home was a beautiful meadow surrounded by lush green woods.

All summer the young seedling grew. Her stem became thick and strong while newly sprouted buds produced perfectly formed leaves. When the days again shortened and cooled, her leaves slowly changed color. One by one, gentle breezes carried them to the ground.

Before dozing off for winter, she admired the tall, straight, beautiful pine trees in the surrounding woods. Though her growth would be different from theirs, her heart filled with gratitude to the Creator that one day she, too, would grow tall and straight and beautiful. No longer Acorn, she was now an Oak.

Seasons came and seasons went. Oak grew from a young sapling into a tall, straight, beautiful tree. Children shared stories and secrets in the shade of her sturdy limbs. Squirrels raced up and down, tickling her trunk. Mama birds built nests high in her branches, hatched their eggs, then watched with pride as their babies learned to fly.

Wind whistling through the surrounding trees created songs that caressed her trunk and leaves. Seeing their branches sway, and feeling her own leaves bouncing in the breeze, Oak was happy to be one of them. Her heart filled with joy that flowed down to her roots and up to the tiniest twigs on her outstretched branches. All was well. She was tall and straight and beautiful. She compared her growth to the surrounding trees and was satisfied. Surely the Creator was satisfied, too.

One morning, the sky turned a sickly gray. Oak shivered. Heavy drops of rain poured from the clouds, soaking the ground. Wind-torn sheets of water stung her trunk and leaves.

A bolt of lightning twisted and cracked through the sky, slashing Oak. Her trunk split into a jagged gash. Waves of bellowing thunder squeezed her exposed heart, and hot steam rose from the ground. Her roots shifted under the altered weight of her shattered trunk, as earthworms burrowed deeper.

Oak stood frozen in terror, wounded and alone. As the storm raged around her, she could not feel her shattered heart. She could not feel her own leaves blowing in the wind or the strength of her roots deep in the ground.

God, will I survive? she gasped, as tears of sap trickled down her splintered trunk. But, she could hear no answer above the noise and confusion.

When the storm's anger was spent, clouds hovered over the meadow in eerie silence. On that day, something in Oak shifted. The connection she felt with the trees and the children and with God vanished. Her branches, now scattered and broken, would no longer shade the children, or be a place where mama birds could build their nests and raise their young. No longer would squirrels race up and down her charred, splintered trunk.

Oak looked at the trees surrounding the meadow. Of all of them, she alone had been wounded. No longer was she the tall, straight, beautiful tree the Creator intended.

Sadness, confusion, and fear consumed her. *How can this be? How can I go on?*

As days became weeks, and weeks became months, and months became years, the lightning that split Oak's heart caused her trunk and branches to grow differently. Though earthworms helped her roots grow strong and deep, with each passing year, her branches became more twisted and awkward.

When thunder rumbled in the distance, Oak feared the lightning would come and strike her again. Feeling her branches tremble, she wanted to crawl back into the ground where the lightning could not find her.

On blustery days, Oak watched the surrounding trees huddle together and imagined their mocking whispers. The wind that stirred their branches no longer created friendly songs. An eerie whistling was all she now heard.

When children came to play in the surrounding woods, Oak shook with sadness! They rarely came to sit in the shade of her branches anymore.

When a child or two walked across the meadow to be with her, she noticed that they seemed to need time to be quiet and think. She understood. She needed time to think as well. Still unable to feel her shattered heart, she wondered if she would ever be whole again.

Oak remembered the day that the lightning cracked through the sky. She remembered the splintering noise and searing pain when it pierced and severed her heart. She remembered standing in the meadow, frozen in terror, wounded and alone.

But, as the years passed, Oak did not know that her shattered heart was altering her growth. Instead, she believed that her deformed branches meant something was very wrong with her. She was ashamed. When Oak looked at the surrounding trees, she saw that God loved beauty and perfection. Because she was no longer beautiful or perfect, she believed God was also ashamed of her.

Every night, Oak prayed to be tall and straight and beautiful. And every day she tried to grow perfectly, so He would be proud of her.

One spring morning, Oak decided that if she could produce the most beautiful leaves, her scar and imperfections would no longer be noticed. If she could produce the most beautiful leaves, more children would come to sit in her shade. Most importantly, if she could produce the most beautiful leaves, they would cover her awkward growth, and God would no longer be ashamed of her. From that day forward, Oak summoned all her strength to produce the most beautiful leaves.

Each spring, as the frozen meadow warmed, she was nudged awake. Immediately, she began pushing and straining. Soon, the tiny buds on her branches and twigs unfurled into leaves and acorns. When caterpillars munched her precious leaves, her limbs shivered with annoyance.

From the moment the first rays of morning sun brushed her trunk, until evening shadows covered the meadow, her leaves opened wide and trapped the sun's energy. Oak used every ounce of that energy creating more beautiful leaves in order to cover her deformed frame.

All summer long, her roots crept wider and deeper. Root hairs absorbed minerals and water, then rushed them through her trunk to feed her branches, twigs, leaves, and acorns.

As autumn breezes wafted over the meadow, Oak used all her strength to create the most glorious display of colors. This, before her leaves fell, and exposed her horrible scar and ugly growth. Each year as sleep overtook her, she prayed for snow to fall and cover her shameful, naked frame.

When winter snow gently covered her barren branches, Oak dreamt of making the following spring her most beautiful and productive year ever.

Oak wished beyond wishing to be tall, straight, and beautiful, but she didn't know how to make her wish come true. And so, with each passing year, she demanded more of herself.

Her work so consumed her, that the birds and squirrels and earthworms which once gave her joy, became an irritating distraction. She no longer noticed or enjoyed the sun and sky and flowers. Eventually, she came to believe that her only true value was in producing the most beautiful leaves of all the trees.

Meanwhile, her weary heart lay shadowed in her trunk with no energy at all.

If a tree works too hard for too long, its heart becomes dried out and it slowly weakens. When Oak began to lose strength and discovered this truth, she became alarmed. *What will happen when my strength is gone? If I cannot produce beautiful leaves, what will the children and trees think of me then? What will God think of me? What use will I be?*

But one day Oak's strength was gone.

All that day, she remained still in frightened silence. When darkness crept over the meadow, questions circled above her branches. *Why can't I be perfect like other trees? Do trees with shattered trunks and awkward growth have value? Do I matter?* In desperation she prayed, *Please God, help me find answers to my questions.* Then exhausted, Oak fell into a deep slumber.

The next day, Oak strained to hear God's answering words. But, He was silent. She waited and listened all day. Still, she did not hear Him.

When evening darkness settled above her branches, new questions circled. *Did God hear me? What if I'm not worth answering? What if God has no answers?*

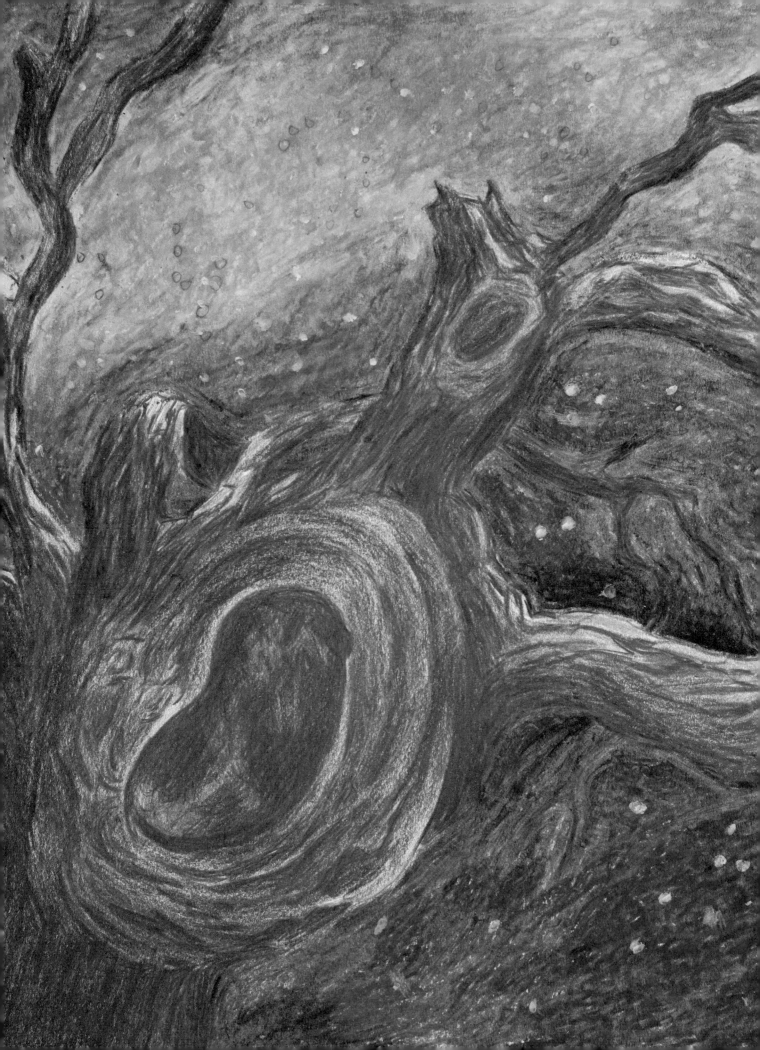

On the third morning, she woke as the sun's warmth kissed her trunk. She sensed God all around her.

Softly He spoke. "Good morning, Oak. Look to the sky on your left."

There she saw a vision of a tree standing alone. A gash split its trunk, and its branches were twisted and bent.

God spoke again, "Now look to the sky on your right."

Shifting her gaze, she saw a vision of a tall, straight, beautiful tree. She admired its perfection and wished she could be like it.

God's voice was gentle. "Now Oak, look back at the tree on your left."

When she looked, God said, "This tree is like you. When the lightning struck you, it split your heart. From that moment on, though you tried to grow like other trees, your trunk and branches were forced to grow differently."

Oak wanted time to think, but God drew her attention back to the tall tree on her right.

"It's beautiful, isn't it?"

His question seemed cruel. The tree's perfect beauty only made her more aware of her own misshapen form. For a moment she was unable to speak. Finally, her whisper agreed, "Yes, it is."

God's voice was kinder than she could have imagined. "Look once more at the tree on your left." As she looked, He asked, "It's beautiful, isn't it?"

Though nothing like the tree on her right, Oak saw how the gash that altered its growth had forged a tree with character. Though its branches were twisted and bent, it had a unique beauty all its own.

Surprised, she heard herself say, "Yes, it is."

In that moment, something in Oak shifted. To think, God was likening her to this tree. Happiness and peace rushed to fill her scar. Instantly, her longing for perfection vanished. For the first time since the lightning struck, she saw her growth as beautiful.

God spoke again. This time he whispered directly into her shattered heart, "When the lightning struck you, I was there. I knew from that moment, your growth would be different. I never expected you to look like other trees. None that has happened is your fault, Oak. I love how you've grown. I think you are beautiful."

God explained, "Every tree I create has a purpose. Some trees have tiny pink flowers, some have big shiny leaves. Some live near the ocean and some live in vast forests. Some trees are like you. They have been injured, and their growth is forever altered. I love all the trees I've ever created, and I love you."

With deep tenderness, God concluded: "My gift to you is life. Be who you are, and love the life you've been given."

Finally, Oak understood. She was free. God loved her. He never wanted her to be who she could not be. He only wanted her to be who she was.

EPILOGUE:

Oak has come to appreciate her unusual growth, and the tree that she is. No longer comparing her growth with that of her uninjured peers, she continues to produce beautiful leaves while reveling in the life she has been given.

In loving memory of my illustrator,
Deborah Knott Walker.

AFTERWORD:

Some years ago, I attended a silent retreat in search of answers to questions about my life that I had never verbalized. At the retreat, I asked God these questions. His answer came to me through a vision that changed my life.

The Riven Tree is an allegorical tale depicting the story of my life prior to receiving the vision. Childhood trauma altered my growth, and the decisions made out of that trauma created judgment and dysfunction in my life. The vision, which I share with the reader, confirmed God's love for me, and, in a moment of insight, grace took the place of judgment in my internal life.

When others heard about the vision, the universal response was, "You need to write a book."

After praying for and receiving direction, the book took shape in my heart. This story has been molded to fit that shape.

My hope is that *The Riven Tree* plants seeds of healing in those whose lives have been affected by trauma, and informs them that they are not alone.

ABOUT THE AUTHOR:

Robby Kautz is a freelance author and women's speaker.

In her story, like that of Oak, violence shattered her heart and altered her growth. Unspoken questions haunted her until God's answer brought hope and healing. *The Riven Tree* shares this message with readers whose hearts and lives have been altered by trauma.

A former interpreter for the Deaf and high school teacher, Robby is married, has two grown children, and lives in Eagle, Idaho.

ABOUT THE ARTIST:

Deborah Knott Walker has a degree in both Art and English Literature from San Francisco State University. For twenty-five years, she taught AP Art, AP Art History, and AP English.

The pencil drawings she has created for *The Riven Tree* are a reflection of her love and passion for all things in nature.

Printed in the United States
By Bookmasters